CANDLE AND CRIB

LECTOR HOUSE PUBLIC DOMAIN WORKS

HAPPY READING!

CANDLE AND CRIB

KATHERINE FRANCES PURDON

ISBN: 978-93-5614-614-3

Published: 1914

LECTOR HOUSE LLP
E-MAIL: info@lectorhouse.com

"AS SOON AS HE WAS GONE, DIDN'T THE WOMAN THROW DOWN
HER KNITTING, AND LAID HER HEAD UPON HER KNEES, AND CRIED"

CANDLE AND CRIB

BY

K. F. PURDON

ILLUSTRATED BY
BEATRICE ELVERY

1914

CONTENTS

CANDLE AND CRIB

CHAPTER I

MOLONEY'S

It would be hard to find a pleasanter, more friendly-looking place in all Arde-noo than Moloney's of the Crooked Boreen, where Big Michael and the wife lived, a piece up from the high-road. And well might you call the little causey "crooked" that led to their door! for rough and stony that *boreen* was, twisting and winding along by the bog-side, this way and that way, the same as if it couldn't rightly make up its mind where it wanted to bring you. So it was all the more of a surprise when you did get to Moloney's, to find a house with such an appearance of comfort upon it, in such a place.

Long and low that house was, and very old. You could tell the great age of it by the thickness of the thatch, as well as by seeing, when you were standing inside upon the kitchen floor and looking up, that that same thatch was resting, not upon common planks, sawn with the grain and against the grain and every way, but upon the real boughs themselves, put there by them that had to choose carefully what would be suitable for their purpose, because there were few tools then for shaping timber. So that's how the branches were there yet, the same as ever, bark and twigs and all; ay, and as sound as the day they were put there, two hundred years before.

As for the walls at Moloney's ... mud, I'm not denying it! but the thickness of them! and the way they were kept white-washed, inside and out! They'd dazzle you, to look at them; especially in the kitchen of an evening, when the fire would be strong. And that was a thing that occurred mostly always at Moloney's. For Herself was a most notorious Vanithee; and there's no better sign of good house-keeping than a clean, blazing hearth. Sure isn't that, as a body might say, the heart of the whole house? Heart or hearth, isn't it all the one thing, nearly? For if warmth and comfort for the body come from the one, doesn't love and pleasant kindness come from the other? Ay, indeed!

And now, here was the Christmas Eve come round again, when every one puts the best foot foremost, whether they can or not. And so by Moloney's. The darkness had fallen, and a wild, wet night it was, as ever came out of the heavens. But that only made the light seem the brighter and more coaxing that the fire was sending out over the half-door, and through the little, twinkling bulls'-eyes windows, as if it was trying to say, "Come along in, whoever you are that's outside in the cold and the rain! Look at the way the Woman has the floor swept, till there isn't a speck upon it! and the tables and stools scoured like the snow, and the big old pewter plates and dishes upon the dresser polished till they're shining like a goat's eyes from under a bed! Come in! Sure every one is welcome here to-night, whether they come or not!"

And still in all...!

Well, one look round would tell you, with half an eye, that something was wrong at Moloney's, Christmas Eve and all as it was. For Big Michael himself was standing there in the kitchen, cracking his red, wet fingers one after the other, and looking most uncomfortable. The wet was running down from his big frieze coat, but it wasn't that he minded. He was too well used to soft weather to care about wet clothes. Beside him upon the floor was the big market-basket, with all manner of paper parcels, blue and brown, sticking out from under the lid that wouldn't shut down, he had brought home so much from Melia's shop. But that basket had a forgotten look about it, because there beside it stood Herself, and she not asking to unpack it or do a thing with it. She was a little bit of a woman, that you'd think you could blow off the palm of your hand with one puff of your breath. As thin as a whip she was, and as straight as a rush; and she was looking up now at Michael with flaming cheeks and eyes like troubled waters.

"No letter!" she was saying; "and is it that you brought home no letter, after you being to the post! Sure it can't be but they wrote to say were they coming or not, after they being asked here for the Christmas! Sure I thought you'd surely have word to say when to expect them; and was thinking even that they might be coming with yourself! Only I suppose the little ass and dray wouldn't be grand enough for the wife! Of coorse I didn't think of *her* writing; she may know no better, and isn't to be blemt if she has no manners; she can't help the way she was brought up! But Art! Sure there must be a letter from him...!"

"Wait and I'll try again!" said Big Michael slowly; and then he took to feel through his pockets again for the letter their son was to have sent them. But when he had done this, he could only shake his head, so that the rain-drops fell from his hair and beard—turning brackety grey, they were, Michael being on in years.

"No, in trath! not as much as one letter have I this night!" he said slowly.

At this the Woman began to laugh, in spite of the great annoyance that was on her.

"Sure," she said, "if Mrs. Melia had a letter for us, wouldn't she have given it to you? What use would *she* have for it? And if she hadn't, and told you so, where's the sense in you feeling your pockets over and over? A body'd think you expected letters to grow there, the same as American apples in barrels! How could you have there what you didn't put there? But let you go on off ou'er this now! Look at the state you have the clean floor in, with the rain dreeping from your *cota-mor!*"

"Coming down it is, like as if it was out of a sieve!" said Michael; "and wasn't it God that done it, that I took the notion to cut the holly'n'ivy while the day was someways fine, afore I started off to the shop! Has it safe below ... so I'll just go for it now, the way we can be settling out the Crib and all ..."

"There'll no holly'n'ivy go up on these walls to-night, if I'm to be let have a say in the business!" said Mrs. Moloney. "Sich trash and nonsense! making mess and trouble for them that has plenty to do without that! And as for the Crib, let it stop where it is ..."

On the word she went back to her stool in the chimney-corner, where she always sat bolt upright, and took up her knitting, the same as if it wasn't the Christmas Eve at all. For Art, their only child, that stocking was meant. But her hands were shaking so much that she dropped more stitches off the needles than she made, and still she persevered. Big Michael looked at her for a bit, very pitiful; even opened his mouth once, as if he wanted to say something; a nice, silent person he was, very even-going in himself. But he must have thought better of it, for he only shook his head again, and turned and went off out of the door into the wild storm and darkness, with the wind howling and threatening all about the bog and country-side, the shockingest ever you knew.

And as soon as he was gone, didn't the Woman throw down her knitting, and laid her head upon her knees, and cried and cried, till her blue checky apron was like as if it was after being wrung out of a tub of suds.

"Och, Art!" she'd cry, "isn't this the queer way for you to be going on! To say you never answered the letter that was wrote to you! This very day five-and-twenty years you came here to us! as lovely as a little angel you were! The grand big blue eyes of you! and the way you'd laugh up at me and put out the little hand...! And you the only one ever God sent us! And never a word between us, only when you took the notion to go off to Dublin; sure it near broke our hearts, but what could we do, only give you our blessing! And ... and then hearing the good accounts of the way you were going on.... But it's the wife that done it all, and has him that changed...! Too grand she is, no doubt, for the likes of us! Och, grand how-are-ye! no, but not half good enough for Art! He that was always counted a choice boy by all that knew him! And any word them that saw the wife beyant in Dublin with him brought back, was no great things. A poor-looking little scollop of a thing, they tell me she is; and like as if she'd have about as much iday of taking butter off a churn, or spinning a hank of yarn, as a pig would have of a holiday! What opinion could any sensible body have of that kind of a wedding, without even a match-maker to inquire into the thing, to see was it anyways suitable or not! Och, Art! Art! it's little I thought, this day five-and-twenty years, the way the thing would be now!"

CHAPTER II
THE STABLE

While poor Mrs. Moloney was fretting like this, and it Christmas Eve and all, Big Michael was making his way through the wind and the sleety rain to where he had his stable, a piece off from the house. It was pitch-dark, so that he couldn't see his hand before his eyes, if he held it up; but he had his lantern, and anyway he knew his way about blindfold. But even in daylight you might pass by that stable ready, unless you knew it was there. For it was very little, and being roofed with heather it looked only like a bit of the bog that had humped itself up a bit higher than the rest.

Poor-looking and small as it was, Big Michael was very proud of that stable. He and Art had built it together, just before Art leaving home. It was wanted to keep the little wad of hay or straw safe from the weather, as well as to shelter the cow of a hard night. And after Art had gone off to the Big Smoke, and for no other reason only getting restless, as young hearts often do, many and many a time Michael would slope off to the stable, and sit down there to take a draw of the pipe and to wish he had his pleasant, active young boy back at home again. He missed Art full as much as the mother, and maybe more.

In fact, it was getting into a habit with Michael to go off to the stable. He had the best of a wife, but still there were times when he'd wish to be with himself somewhere, so that he could take his ease, and still not be feeling himself an annoyance to a busy woman. Big Michael himself, the people said, always looked as if he thought to-morrow would do. But the Woman that owned him was of a different way of thinking, always going at something. So he got the fashion of keeping out of her way.

When he got to the stable this night, a bit out of breath with the great wind, he took notice first of the cow, and he saw that she was comfortable, plenty of straw to lie upon, and plenty of fodder before her. So then he bethought him of the little ass that was outside under the dray yet.

"I'll put her in too!" he thought. "Destroyed she is and quite weakly with the wet, like all donkeys, God help them! let alone the mud and gutter she's after travelling through, all that long ways from the shop! And carrit the things we were in need of, too! I'll let her stand here near the cow. A good dry bed I'll put under her, and give her a grain of oats to pet her heart. It'll not go astray with her, and she has it well earned, the creature!"

So he unyoked the ass and led her into the stable, and rubbed down her shaggy coat, all dripping like his own clothes, and fed her, and watched with a curious satisfaction the nice way, like a lady, that she took the feed he put before her.

"Poor Winny!" he said, rubbing a finger up and down her soft ears; "many's the time Art laughed at you, and said it was only one remove from a wheel-barra to be driving you! Ling-gerin' Death is what he used to call you! But sure you do your best! and if you were the fastest horse ever won the Grand National, you could do no more!"

He looked round then, with a very satisfied feeling. There he had them, the two poor animals that depended out of him, but that served him and his so well, too; had them safe and warm from the storm and rain outside. He swung the lantern to and fro, so that he could see everything that was in the stable. One end of it was filled with hay and straw. The light gleamed here, gleamed there upon the kind, homely plenty he had stored. Then it fell upon a heap of something else; something that glistened from many points, green and cheerful.

"The holly'n'ivy," Big Michael thought, "that I cut this morning, and has it here, the way it would be handy to do out the place in greenery against Art and the wife would be here! Well, well! I wouldn't wish to go against Herself, and she so fretted; but sure I might as well not have cut it at all!"

He stood and stared at it, very mournful in himself. For the best part of the Christmas to Michael was not the good feeding Herself always provided, though he could take his share of that, as well as another; no, but the holly and ivy and the Candle and the Crib; and now she had set her face against them all. And it wouldn't be Christmas at all, he thought, without them!

A sudden thought came into his mind.

"Why can't I have it Christmas here," he said to himself, "and not be letting all these beautiful green branches go to waste! That's what I'll do!"

And with that, he laid down the lantern, and began to decorate the little stable. He moved slowly, but the work grew under his hands. He put the bright, glistening holly in the rack that the cow fed from, and over the door. And he flung the long curving trails of ivy over the rafters, so that they hung down, and the whole place became the most loveliest bower of green that you might ask to see.

He had just put up the last of his green stuff, when the lantern flickered up and then quenched; it was burnt out.

"Dear, dear!" thought Michael; "a pity it is to say there's no light to see it by; even if there's no one to look at it, itself!"

He stood still a bit. It always took Michael a good while even to think. Then he said to himself, "Wait a bit! go aisy, now, will ye!" as if the wife was there to be prodding him on. And then he began slowly to unbutton his coat, and then another under that, and another, and so on, much like peeling skins off an onion, till at last he came to something that he drew out very carefully; something long and slim, and that gleamed white in the light of a match he struck against the wall.

"BIG MICHAEL CONTRIVED TO LIGHT THE CANDLE"

"*There's* a Christmas Candle for ye!" he said, looking admiringly at it; "two foot long if it's an inch! Mrs. Melia does the thing right, if she goes to do it at all, the decent nice poor woman that she is! Gave me that Candle in a Christmas present; her Christmas box she said it was, and says she, 'It'll do to welcome Art and the young wife home!' says she. And so of course it would, if only it was a thing that they were coming.... But sure, God knows what happened to stop them.... But I thought it as good say nothing about the Candle, foreninst Herself, to be making her worse, when I seen the way she was about the Crib itself! It's a pity she not to see it ..."

Slowly and awkwardly Big Michael contrived to light the Candle and to set it up in a bucket that was there handy. He steadied it there by melting some of the grease around it, and made it firm so that it could not upset to do damage to the stable. Then when it was burning well he went off, turning when he got out into the storm and darkness outside to look again at the Candle that was shedding a ray of lovely light far into the night.

"Ay, indeed!" thought he to himself, with great satisfaction, "it is a grand fine Christmas Candle, sure enough! And it would be noways right for us, even if we are only with ourselves to-night, not to have one lit, the same as every other house in Ardenoo has, the way if any poor woman with a child in her arms was wandering by, far from her own place, she'd see the light and know there was room and a welcome waiting there for them both! Ay, indeed! a great Candle that is, and will last well and shine across the whole bog! But I wish Mrs. Melia had given me the letter as well!"

CHAPTER III
THE LETTER

The queer thing is that Big Michael, slow and all as he was, happened to be right about the letter from Art. It had been written, and, moreover, it had reached Ardenoo post-office. But no one knew that for certain, or what became of it, only a small little pup of a terrier dog belonging to one of the Melia boys. This pup was just of an age that it was a great comfort to his mouth to have something he could chew. He was lying taking his ease, just under the counter where the letters got sorted. And when, as luck would have it, Art's letter slipped down, of all others! from the big heap of papers and all sorts that came very plenty at that Christmas season, this little dog had no delay, only begin on the letter. In two minutes he had "little dan" made of it!—nothing left of it only a couple or three little wet rags that got swep' out the next morning, and never were heard of again. Sure, why would they, when only the pup knew anything about them? And he couldn't explain the thing, even if he had wanted to. He escaped a few kicks by that. Still, dogs often get into trouble the same way, God help them! without having earned it at all.

Yes, the invitation for the Christmas was answered. The wife, Delia her name was, had said nothing at first when it came. To tell the truth, she was well satisfied where she was, with Art and the child all to herself, in their one room in a back street. Up a lot of stairs it was, too, and the other people in the house not to say too tasty in their way of going on. But poor Delia thought it was all grand, with the little bits of furniture herself and Art would buy according as they could manage it, and the cradle in the corner by the fire.

Poor Art would smother there betimes, nigh-hand, when he'd think of the Crooked Boreen, and the wide silence of the bog, with the soft sweet wind blowing across it, and the cows and all, and the neighbours to pass the time of day with, let alone the smell of the turf-fire of an evening! Homesick the poor boy was, and didn't know it.

The way it came about that Art left home was, he got tired of things there, the very things he wanted now. And there was some said, the mother was too good and fond with him. She'd lay the two hands under his feet any hour of the day or night; thought the sun shone out of him, so she did. And Art was always good and biddable with her; never gave any back-talk, or was contrary. But all the time he wanted to be himself. He was much like a colt kept in a stall, well fed and minded, but he wants to get out to stretch his legs in a long gallop all the time.

So there's why Art went off from Ardenoo to the Big Smoke, and got on the best ever you knew. He was very apprehensive about machinery, could understand it well, and got took on by a great high-up doctor to mind his motor for him. The old people were that proud when they heard of it.

"Sure it's on the Pig's Back Art is now, whatever!" they said, "with his good-lookin' pound a week!"

Wealth that sounded, away off in Ardenoo. But the sorra much spending there is in it in a city, where you're paying out for everything you want. Delia did the best she could with it, but it wouldn't do all she wanted.

Still, she pleased Art. Small and white in the face she was, as Mrs. Moloney had imagined her. Sewing she used to be, a bad life for a girl to be at it all day. But she flourished up well after getting married. And what Art had looked into, when he was courting, was the big, longing-looking dark eyes of her, and the gentle voice and ways, and the clouds of soft brown hair ... well, sure every eye forms a beauty of its own. But Art might have done worse nor to marry Delia Fogarty that never asked to differ from a word he said, till the notion came up of they going to Ardenoo for the Christmas. When the letter asking them came, he near riz the roof off the house, the shout he gave, he was that delighted in himself to be going back home.

"But what's a trouble to you, Delia?" he says, when he had time to take notice that she wasn't looking as rejoiced as he expected, only sitting there with her eyes upon the child in her arms; "a body'd think you didn't care about going at all!" he says, half vexed.

"I ... I'd like to go, Art," says Delia, "only I don't know do I want to go or not.... I ... do you see ..."

"Well ... what?"

"Sure ... maybe ... how do I know will they like me or not! And me coat all wore ... and ... and, moreover, I never got to get a right sort of a hood for the child ... or a cloak...."

"Och, what at all, girl dear!" says Art, that was so excited at the thoughts of getting home that nothing was a trouble to him; "not like you! What else would they do! And the child ... well, now, isn't it well we told them nothing about him, the way he'll be a surprise to them now? The fine big fellah that he is! Sure it would be a sin to go put any clothes on him at all, hiding the brave big legs of him!"

Delia had to laugh at that; and then Art went out and bought a grand sheet of note-paper with robins and red berries and "The Season's Compliments" at the top of it. And Delia wrote the letter upon this, because she could write real neat and nice. Art told her every word to say.

> Dear Father and Mother, it began, "I have pleasure in taking up my pen to rite yous those few lines hopping they find yous in good health as they leave us at this present thank you and God. I would wish my love and best wishes to..." and there were so many to be remembered that Art told Delia to put in "all inquiring friends," and even shortened like that, the list hardly left room for

saying, "and we will go home for the Christmas and is obliged for the kindness of asking and we will go by the last train Christmas Eve and let yous meet that with Ling-gerin' Death and the cart and we're bringing a Christmas box wid us that yous will be rejoiced to see so I will end those few lines from your

"SON AND NEW DAUGHTER."

When that letter was finished and posted, Delia made no more of an objection to going, only did the best she could, washing and mending her own little things and the baby's. But let her do her best and they were poor-looking little bits of duds! And many's the time, when Art was away, that she'd cry, and wish to herself that there was no such a place as Ardenoo on the face of this earthly world. But what could she do, only please Art!

Well, the very evening before they were to start for Ardenoo, didn't Art come home to her in great humour. "Look at here, Delia!" says he, with a big laugh; "see the fine handful of money," and he held it out to her, "that Himself is after giving me in a Christmas box! Now we'll do the thing in real style! Come along out now, before the shops shut, and we'll buy all before us!"

Well, if you were to see the two of them that night! the three, indeed, for Delia wouldn't ever leave the child, only took him with her. To see them looking in at the grand bright windows full of things! and going in, Delia half afraid, but Art as loud and outspoken as a lord, spending free as long as it lasted! To see him then going home with her and the child, and he all loaded down with parcels! and opened them all out, the minute they got back! All the things they bought out of that money! A pipe and tobacco for Michael; a lovely cake with "Merry Christmas" in pink sugar upon it, for Herself; the grandest of brown shoes and a hat and feather for Delia, and as for the baby!... Delia could scarce believe her eyes, all they had got for him, things she had been wanting....

Art made her fit them all on, and when she held up the child to be admired, with the loveliest of a soft white shawl rolled round him, "He becomes it well," says Art; "and I suppose you think to make him look better nor he is, by all that finery!"

"Your mother'll think him terrible small," said Delia, looking very fretted again; but she kissed the baby, as much as to say, "Little I care what she thinks!"

She said nothing about that part of it, though, only looked up at Art with the beseeching eyes I mentioned before.

"Let that go round!" says Art; and he lifted the two of them in his arms and kissed them both; and then when he had let Delia go, says he, "Me mother is the smallest little crathureen herself, that ever you saw! So she needn't talk! And sure what can you expect from a child not a month old yet! And there's an ould saying and a true one, in Ardenoo, 'It's not always the big people that reaps the harvest!' and so by this boy of ours! We won't feel till he'll be working!"

"Working!" said Delia. And she unclasped the baby's fingers and kissed the tiny hands inside, that were as soft and pink as rose-leaves, first one hand and then the other. She never thought that every hand, no matter how rough and strong, begins by being a baby's hand like the one she was after kissing.

HE KISSED THEM BOTH

"Ay, work!" says Art, very determined; "it would amaze you or any one that didn't know, the way the children grow up and get sense at Ardenoo! the way if the old people seemed wishful for us to stop at home with them, this little fellah of ours would soon ... but whisht!" before poor Delia had time to say a word one way or other about this iday, "whisht! what's this at all! A telegram! for me!"

A telegram! Poor Delia turned gashly pale at the word, and hugged the child closer to her, as if she thought that little bit of an orange-coloured envelope might be going to do some destruction on her treasure.

Art read it slowly to himself, while his face grew as long as to-day and to-morrow; and says he, "Well, it can't be helped! The Master that's after getting a hurried call to the country and will want me to drive him ... so I'll not be at read'ness to go...." He looked anxiously at Delia.

Not go to Ardenoo! Delia's heart leaped up.

"Sure, can't we stop where we are?" says she, with dancing eyes.

"Och, not at all!" says Art; "it wouldn't answer at all to be disappointing them. And besides, it's down that side he wants to go ... some sick child ... the Master I mean ... I'll likely be at Ardenoo before you!"

"But, Art! ... is it go wid meself? What will I do at all at all?" and Delia begins to cry.

"See here now," says Art, "don't be taking on, that way! You wouldn't have me disappoint the Master ... after he being so good to us, too! The fine grand little clothes we're after getting!... You'll be as right as rain! Just wait till you're at Ardenoo, where every one knows me! Why, you'll be with friends, that very minute! And you wrote it in the letter yourself, what train to meet you at.... You wouldn't be fretting me mother and she thinking to have us for the Christmas ... to make no mention of the child at all!"

"To be sure not!" says Delia. And she dried her eyes and said no more, only got ready and went off the next day with the little child, as smiling and gay as she could appear, waving her hand to Art that saw her off at the Broadstone station, and did all he could to put her in heart. But it's a long, long ways from the Big Smoke to Ardenoo. Hours and hours it took that wet, wild day to get there. And Delia wasn't too well accustomed to trains and going about. She managed to keep the child warm and comforted all through, but when the train stopped at Ardenoo she was that tired and giddy herself, that she scarcely knew what she was doing or where she was to go.

She stood a minute on the platform, with the wind and rain beating down upon her, till it had her even more confused. And the day was nearly done, and no lamps lit yet. But she made out a porter and asked him, as Art had bid her, for Mr. Moloney's ass-cart.

"Moloney's ass and dray? Ay," says the man, "Big Michael was in the Town to-day at Melia's, and buying all before him, by what I hear. And not too long ago it was ..."

"Would I ... could I find him ... where's that place you're after mentioning?"

And Delia took a grip of the big hat, that the wind was getting at.

"Melia's shop? You can't miss it! There's ne'er another.... He should have left it by now ... but let you go on along that road ..." and he showed her where it lay, stretching off into the darkness, "and you'll overtake him, ready! That ass is middling slow!"

The man guessed who this was speaking to him, for they all had heard about Art and the wife being expected for the Christmas. And he had no call to tell her to go off like that. Big Michael was nigh-hand at home again by then. But he had a sup taken at that present, as often happens at Christmas. Only he was a bit "on," he'd never have put such an iday into Delia's head. To think of letting her start after Michael like that!

But poor Delia knew no better than to follow fool's advice; how could she? So she just asked some directions about the road, and then she changed the child from one arm to the other and faced out in the night and rain, and a wind that would blow the horns off a goose to overtake the ass-cart. Little she thought that it was back at the Crooked Boreen by then, near five good miles away!

For a while, she wasn't in too bad a heart at all. She was glad to be out of the train, and she was expecting every step to get some signs of Michael on in front. But the little light there was went altogether before long; quenched, like, by the great rain and the heavy clouds that hung low and dark in the skies. Delia began to feel it very lonesome! But she kept going on; what else could she do?

At this time, what she thought worst of was, that the wet was spoiling her good hat, after Art spending his money upon it, the way she could make some kind of appearance foreninst his mother and the neighbours. But what could she do to save it?

"The cut I'll be!" she thought; "all dreeped with rain!" And indeed the hat, with its grand feather all broken and draggled, was a poor-looking thing enough before she was half-ways to the Crooked Boreen. As for the grand shoes with the high heels, they were like sponges upon her feet, and she slipping in them as she stumbled along through mud and gutter to her ankles.

But she kept going on! The baby lay warm and snug upon her heart. She managed to keep him sheltered, anyway! Now and then she'd stop and put her face down to his, to feel his sweet warm breath upon her cheek. Then she'd go on again. That ass-cart! If only she could catch it! Wouldn't it be Heaven to be taken off her aching feet and be carried along, herself and the child, with some one that knew the way, and not to be feeling lost, as she did now.

For by degrees that's what Delia had to think; she was lost. Still she struggled on, the poor little bet-down thing that she was; so tired that she only kept moving at all by clenching her teeth hard and saying out loud, "I must! I must! A nice thing it would be for Art to not find me when he gets home! I must keep going on! The baby would die if I was to lie down ..." for that is what she was more inclined for than anything else.

The wind was coming in great gusts now, hindering her far worse than the rain. It caught her skirts like the sails of a ship; it snatched at her hat. She tried to hold it on, but a sudden strong blast came, just as she was shifting the child again in her arms. Like a spiteful hand, it tore the hat from her head and furled it away; and what could be done, to get it again, in the storm and darkness? Delia cried at first, thinking of the loss it was. But she minded nothing long, only the tiredness and that still she must keep going on.

Suddenly she began to sing to the child:

> I laid my love in a cradley-bed,
> *Lu lu lu lu la lay.*
> Little white love with a soft round head,
> *Lu lu lu lu la lay.*

Before she had it done, she thought to see a light a piece off from her. She made towards it. Out upon the bog itself she was now; and them that saw her tracks after, said one of the holy Angels must have been guiding her then, that she wasn't drownded, herself and the child, in a bog-hole. She slipped here and she fell there on the wet, rough ground; but she kept on till she reached the light. It was the Christmas Candle, in Michael's stable, burning there, mild and watchful.

CHAPTER IV

THE CRIB

While all this was going on, Big Michael was sitting, snug and comfortable, in the chimney-corner, opposite the wife, and she knitting, knitting away still. Not a word was passing. She had Michael's supper ready for him, hot and tasty, the same as ever. But he had no *goo* for it. What did he care was it good or bad! How could he feel gay and riz up in himself, the way a body should at the Christmas, when he knew well Herself had been crying away while he had been down at the stable?

If only she'd cheer up! If only she'd agree to have the place dressed out, and the Crib and all the other little things done the same as ever! It would do herself good, and they might be having a happy Christmas after all, even if there was only the two of them there with themselves! But he said nothing. Big as Michael was, and little as the Woman was that owned him, it was she had the upper hand in the house. And good right, too; she being a very understanding person, and considered to be a good adviser of a woman all over Ardenoo. Michael was slow, but he was wise enough to give in to the wife. So now when she showed no wish for any of the things he was so made upon, he said no more about them; only after a while says he, "I believe it's what I'll take a streel off to see is the cow all right in the stable below...."

But what he really wanted was, to get away from the queer, unhappy feel of the silent kitchen. He thought, too, he'd like another sight of the dressed-out stable and the big Candle he had lit there. He meant to stop a bit with those Christmas signs, and the ass, and the munch, munch of the cow, filling the place with her fragrant breath.

Wasn't it a pity of the world that Herself was having none of the pleasure? If only he could tell her what he had been doing! If only he could get her to come too, and see how lovely the stable looked!

As he passed out on the door, the Vanithee looked after him. A kind of pity rose warm in her heart, as she saw the fretted appearance was upon the big man, like a cowed dog, with his tail drooping between his legs.

All the bygone Christmas Eves they had put in there together! Kind, pleasant times, with little old nonsense and laughing, that no one understood, only themselves! Art had been there, to be sure! He had been the delight of the first of their Christmases, and the same always, till he went off. But was it Michael's fault that the son wasn't there yet? Sure poor Michael had done nothing to fret her! It wasn't he had neglected to write! And wasn't it full as bad for him, Michael, that had always been the fond father to Art! and had never rightly overed the boy's quitting off the way he did! Oh, if only they had Art there again! To have him going off with the father of a morning, cutting turf, or making hay, or doing a bit of ploughing! and the two of them in to their dinners and off again!... Why, to have that good time back, she'd even welcome the poor-lookin' little scollop of a thing, and give her share of the old home!...

Poor Michael! He that loved the Christmas! Like a child, he was! Most men are, if they have any good in them; and God help them if they get a woman that doesn't understand that, and can't make allowances when they don't grow up!

Mrs. Moloney was as quick as Michael was slow. So, while he'd be thinking about it, she had a stool over at the dresser and was up on it, feeling for the Crib on the top shelf.

It was there, safe enough, and it wrapped in a newspaper. A small little contraption of a thing it was, that she had bought off Tommy the Crab, the peddling man, years before. Paid sixpence for it, too; and cheap he told her it was at that money.

To see it first, it was no more than a middling sizeable Christmas card. But it was really in three, or maybe four, halves that drew out like a telescope. The first part showed the Kings kneeling with their offerings and crowns upon their heads; then you could see the Shepherds, with their crooks and they kneeling too; and in the middle of them all, the Mother herself, with the Holy Child upon her knee. St. Joseph was at one side, and the ox and the ass at the other; all complete, even to a grand Star of silver paper, shining on the top of it all.

Mrs. Moloney put the Crib into one of the small square windows and drew it out. Then she went back to the dresser for the candles to light it up with. It looked nothing wanting them.

Not common candles she was going to use, but what had been blessed at Candlemas, and that she had kept put by very carefully.

"I mustn't take them all," she thought, "the way, if one of us was to take and die sudden, there would be a Candle ready to put into the dying hand, to light the soul on its way! But there's a good few, and so ..."

Four she took for the four evangelists, and was just lighting them up, when suddenly the door burst open, and with a rush and a laugh in came ... Art!

"Mother!" he said; and in a moment had his arms round her, and was kissing her lips.

"Oh, Art! so you did come, after all!" says she, with a catch in her breath and a gush of joy to her heart. She had her son, her own son again! And for a minute she forgot everything else—the missed letter, Art's wife....

"Come? And why wouldn't I come? What else? Och, but it's grand, the smell of the turf! And the Crib the same as ever! Och, mother, mother! But where's Delia? Some tricks you and her is up to! Has them hid 'on' me? Delia! Delia! where at all are you?"

THE MOTHER WITH HER CHILD LYING VERY STILL

At that the mother drew a piece away from him. Her face that had been smiling and rosy even, like a girl's face, grew stiff and white.

"Delia! Delia! he can think of nothing else," she thought. It all came back upon her, like a bad dream. Her son had a wife now! And she had held out her hand to them, and they had slighted it!

What did Art mean, coming in like a strong wind? Gay and pleasant as summer air at first, but his face changed and became black and stormy and his voice was a strange, fierce voice, asking again, "Where's Delia?"

"I know nothing about her! How could I?"

"Sure she was to be here ..."

"We got no word ..."

"No word! Is it that no one met them at the train? My God! what has become of her and the child? And the night it was!"

The child? What child? the mother was trying to ask, but the words were stopped on her lips, and Art was stopped at the door, in his mad rush forth to look for his wife and baby, by the appearance before them of Michael. Stopped them both, I say, but without a word being spoken. It was just the look in the old man's face that made them both fall back a step and stand still, looking at Michael in a sort of wonder and fright. His eyes were shining, as if he had been in another world, and had scarcely got back to earth again. He stood facing them for a minute with the same far-away look; then he took each of them by the hand, and just breathed out, "Come! come with me and see what's in the stable ..."

They went. The wind had fallen and the rain had ceased. A beautiful moon had risen, and was shining, but you could not see her, only the light she shed down from her throne on high through the soft white mist that had risen from the wet ground and was wavering and dancing solemnly to and fro, filling the space between heaven and earth, as if to veil the sacred sights of the Holy Eve from mortal eyes. The father and mother and son moved silently through the misty, gleaming silence, till they reached the stable, where the Candle was burning steadily, and sending forth its pure white light into the moonlit vapour.

Michael stepped on and was at the door first. He put his great arm across, as if to ensure caution and reverence.

"Go easy, go easy, the both of yous! but sure, they might be gone back already, and no one to have seen them, only meself!" he said in the same awed whisper.

They peered in, for beyond the Candle were dusky spaces; yet its light was enough to show them two figures there; a girl-mother with her child, lying very still.

Was she asleep, or.... She was so white and small! The long dark hair had been loosened and fell about her like a soft mantle; and close, close to her heart lay the little child.

"Delia, Delia!" said Art.

"The Child!" said his mother.

Delia unclosed her eyes and looked up with a little smile. "I have him here, safe!" she said.

And Michael, only half comprehending, fell on his knees and sobbed aloud.

THE END

Lector House believes that a society develops through a two-fold approach of continuous learning and adaptation, which is derived from the study of classic literary works spread across the historic timeline of literature records. Therefore, we aim at reviving, repairing and redeveloping all those inaccessible or damaged but historically as well as culturally important literature across subjects so that the future generations may have an opportunity to study and learn from past works to embark upon a journey of creating a better future.

This book is a result of an effort made by Lector House towards making a contribution to the preservation and repair of original ancient works which might hold historical significance to the approach of continuous learning across subjects.

HAPPY READING & LEARNING!

LECTOR HOUSE LLP
E-MAIL: info@lectorhouse.com